P9-CCO-338
BELMONT PUBLIC LIBRARY

For my teacher and friend, Marie Campbell,
who taught me how to listen
—K.D.

For Lydia, Tommy, Ben, Oskar & Teddy
—Z.O.

POE WON'T GO

WRITTEN BY
KELLY DiPUCCHIO

ILLUSTRATED BY
ZACHARIAH OHORA

DISNEY • HYPERION
Los Angeles New York

One morning, the good people of Prickly Valley awoke to find an elephant sitting smack-dab in the middle of the only road in town.

How he got there was a mystery. His name was Poe.

It didn't take long for a traffic jam to form around the uninvited elephant. Horns honked. People yelled from their cars. A policeman wrote him a ticket.

But Poe wouldn't go.

So the good people of Prickly Valley took to banging pots and pans to shoo him away.

They blew trombones and blasted megaphones.

They tugged, and tickled, and tap-danced.

But Poe wouldn't go.
The crowd grew larger and louder.
People begged.

And booed. **JEEZ!**

And bribed. CHEESE?

But Poe *still* wouldn't go.

As the day wore on, the townspeople grew more clever.

They brought in mice . . .

and magnets . . .

and motivational speakers.

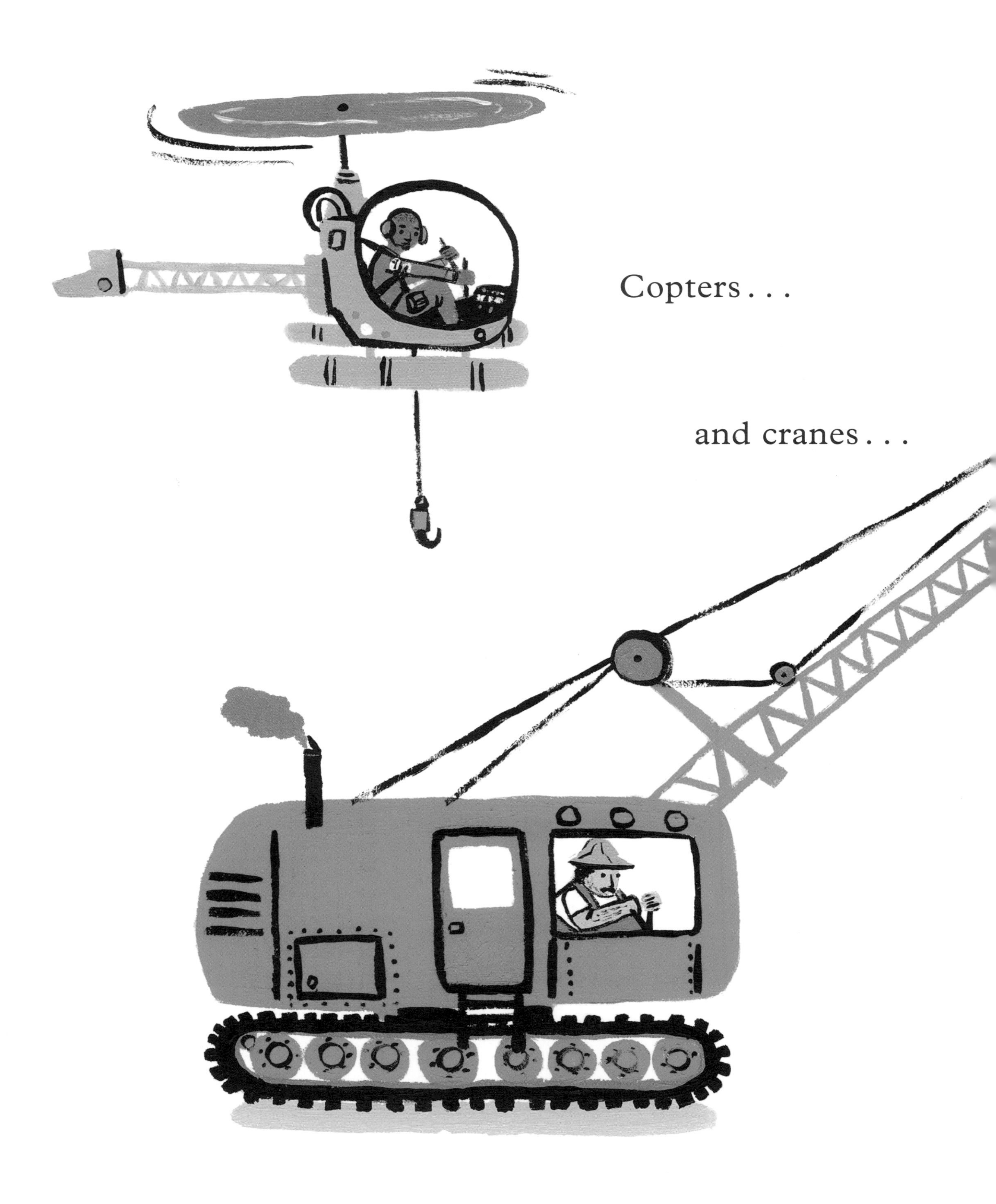

Copters . . .

and cranes . . .

and clowns with horn squeakers.

But there wasn't a pastor or plow in town who knew how to get Poe to go.

THE AMAZING CARL
MAGIK LIFTS

Not even The Amazing Carl could make the elephant disappear.

Finally, the mayor arrived on the scene.

"We do not tolerate parked pachyderms in Prickly Valley!" she proclaimed.

The mayor formed committees and councils.
They hatched plans. Drew diagrams.
And drank coffee from Styrofoam cups.

By late afternoon the entire town of Prickly Valley
and the neighboring village of Ottersville
all lined up behind the stubborn elephant.

Remarkably, that plan failed as well.

As did this one.

And that one.

Nope. Nothing doing.

Seriously?

The townspeople were fresh out of ideas.

And Poe? Well . . . you know.

A girl named Marigold approached the mayor.
"Excuse me, ma'am.
Has anyone asked Poe *why* he won't go?"

"*Ask him?* Child! The good people of Prickly Valley do not speak elephant!"

"Well, anyone can speak elephant if they just listen hard enough," said Marigold, who was fluent in both kitten and hedgehog.

The girl climbed a ladder,
pressed her ear to Poe's forehead,
and closed her eyes.

Marigold concentrated.
A minute passed before she addressed the crowd.
"He said he's waiting for a friend," she announced.
"And his friend is very late."

"That's preposterousssss!" hissed the mayor.
"You're making that up!"

A news reporter chimed in. "Hey, kid!
Can you ask the elephant if, by chance,
his friend is wearing a polka-dot tie?"

Marigold leaned into the elephant for a second time.

"Someone remove that silly girl!" the mayor snapped. "It's getting late, and this is a waste of precious—"

Marigold interrupted the mayor's rant. "He said it's possible."

The news reporter chuckled.

"Well, then it's possible this elephant is SITTING on his friend!"

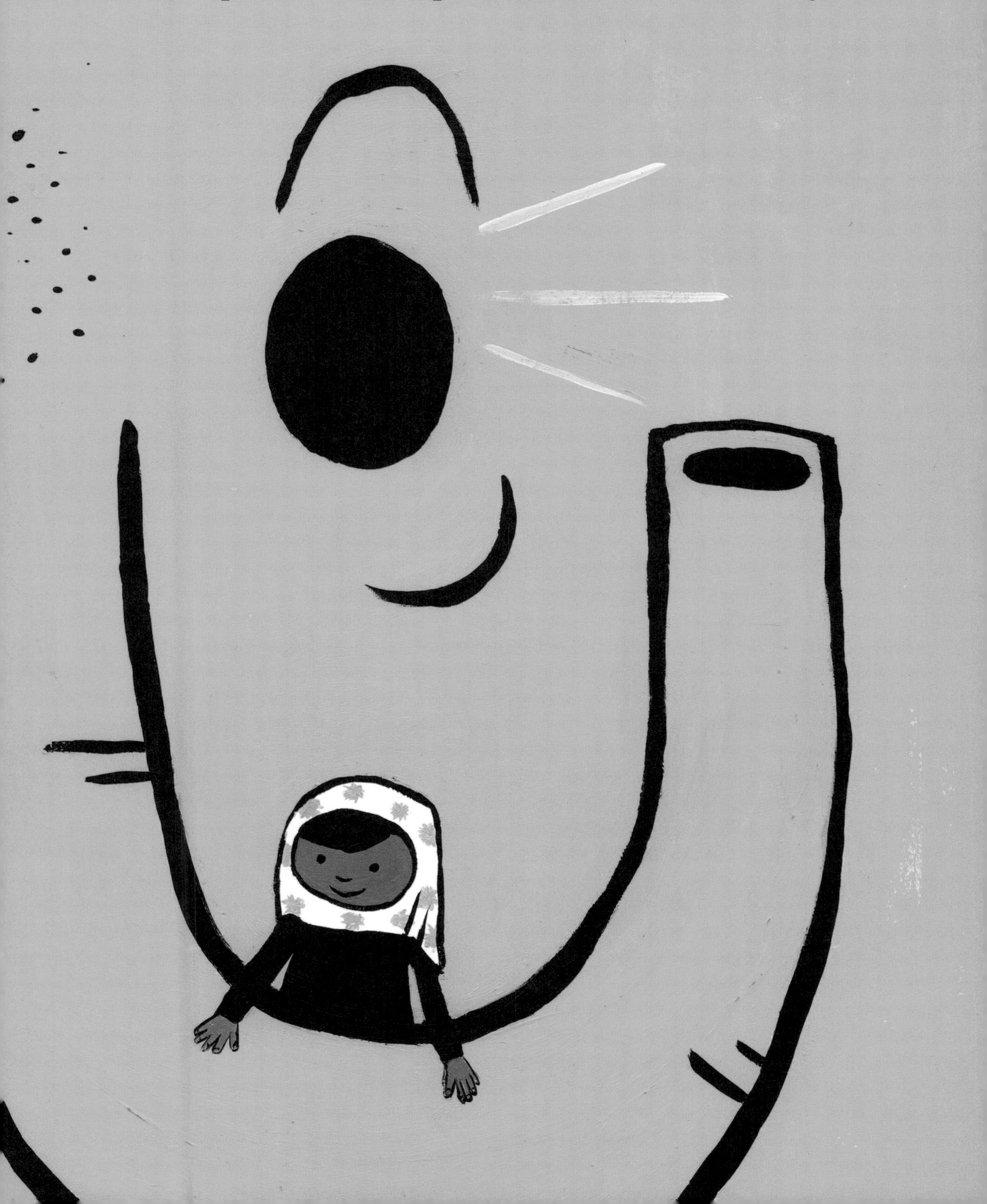

And just like that, Poe got up. And he went.

With his friend, Moe.

I wonder where they'll go?